T0158993

ADVENTURES AT LASAGNA PREPOPERP

Dedicated to
Ethan "Bunkey" Gabriel Weaver

ADVENTURES AT LASAGNA PREPOPERP

KEVIN WEAVER

ADVENTURES AT LASAGNA PREPOPERP

iUniverse books may be ordered through booksellers or by contacting:

iUniverse
1663 Liberty Drive
Bloomington, IN 47403
www.iuniverse.com
1-800-Authors (1-800-288-4677)

ISBN: 978-1-5320-6313-8 (sc)
ISBN: 978-1-5320-6312-1 (e)

Library of Congress Control Number: 2019902841

Print information available on the last page.

iUniverse rev. date: 03/06/2019

CHAPTER 1

The Beginning

Welcome to Lasagna Prepoperp
Watch Out for Palindromes!

Dear Reader,

Hello. My name is Thom T. Moht. I am the lefty class president here at Lasagna Preparatory Relational Environmental Plenipotentiary of Perpetual Educational Readiness Placement (now that's a mouthful). To simplify, we just go by Lasagna Prepoperp.

There is another class president (we have two classes here). His name is Neil A. Nalien. Neil leads the righties. Our mascot here at Lasagna Prepoperp is the hog. Hence we are the Lasagna Hogs. Don't laugh. We could have been a flower—ew! A werewolf? Wow!

In case you are wondering where the name Lasagna came from, allow me to elaborate.

The community we live in is the Village of Lasagna. Our little hamlet is situated snugly between Lake Ontario and Lake Erie in northwestern New York State. Our quaint settlement is a small farming community. The plush verdant countryside was settled by two immigrant Italian families: the Cosmo Lazags and the Otis Onias. Upon completion of their part of the Erie Canal, which runs through the village, the two stonemasons were such good friends they decided that they should incorporate. They mashed their names together, and—*voilà*—the Village of Lasagna was born.

You also need to know that everyone here at Lasagna Prepoperp shares the same major: "Getting outa Here 101." We all want out, you know, like Scooby-Doo used to say— "Oh my gorsh! Let's *G-O D-O-G*!" Please don't judge; we don't want to be here any more than I bet you want to be at your school. But od ot tahw?

Oh yeah, and sometimes we say things backward around here. Look for the obvious, and read it backward. Then "od ot tahw?" reads "What to do?"

What should we do? You tell me. Here's a little advice to help you along, not only in school but in life: "Make the best of things." You know, like "If life hands you a nomel, make nomel ade." Figure it out?

Here's another tidbit (or *tibdit*, if you choose). As you seek not only the obvious, look for phrases or words less conspicuous, like my name, Thom T. Moht. My name spelled backward or forward is the same. My name is a palindrome.

Incidentally, Neil's full name is a palindrome as well: Neil A. Nalien. Try it!

From here forward, I will try to italicize all palindromes as a clue, but you're on your own for the backward ones that aren't palindromes. From here on out, I will not take the time to unscramble the easily perceptible ones. I will leave that up to you.

In addition (not subtraction—that's for another day), try to identify other forms of fun language, like onomatopoeia (that's fun to say). Or make up words of your own. At any rate, just have fun reading this stuff.

Emordnilap,
Thom T. Moht

PS—Some people have already said that I may have used words that are too hard for you to understand. Well then, Googlegoog it! Or you can look them up in a dictionary. Remember dictionaries?

PSS—*Emordnilap* is not a made-up word. Look it up.

PSSS—I've been asked what my middle initial, *T,* stands for. It's a bit complicated, but here goes. *T* stands for— what else?—*Terrific*! *Terrific* backward is *cifirret*. Spelled backward, *cifirret* is *terrific*. Don't look it up; you will not find a definition. However, the word *ferritic* is a valid word for Scrabble. It's worth thirteen points.

See y'all at the end!

CHAPTER 2

Campus Life

Go Hang a Salami!

Now then, getting back to life on campus at Lasagna Prepoperp. Not only does everyone here have the same mission, but we share the same food. Everyone eats the same thing every day. No menu. No choices ... just salami. Yep! You heard me right—*imalas*. (Don't forget—read it backward.)

We eat salami everything. We eat so much salami I beg you please ask me, "How much salami do you eat?" Let me tell you ... We eat salami-stuffed breakfast burritos, slices of salami in our salami sack lunches, super salami snacks, and chunks of salami in our supercilious (because salami rules, LOL), su-per-ca-li-fra-gi-lis-tic-ex-pi-a-li-do-cious (you guessed it), super-syllabification, scrumpdillyocious alphabet soup for supper. There is so much salami around here that we made the salami a key part of our school motto: "Go hang a salami; I'm a Lasagna Hog!"

I'll bet dimes to doughnuts that someone just thought, *What in the world does it mean to "hang a salami"?* I am so pleased you asked.

Now, on to chapter 3. Chapter 3 is what I call a parenthetical chapter. It is a chapter that leaves the plot of the story for just a moment so I can describe what it means to hang a salami.

Hanging a salami is a critical part of a video game that we all play, *The Leaning Tower of Pizza*. The game doesn't exist in reality; by *reality*, I mean outside of this book. It is purely a prototype ... perhaps. Fictional. An idea. A thought. A dream ... an imagination. Maybe somebody, someday, someway, will take it to create it.

Off we go ...

CHAPTER 3

The Leaning Tower of Pizza

(Parentheses)

Go Hang a Salami is the subtitle and nugatory (not really necessary, just for fun) plot of a video game we created here at Lasagna Prepoperp. Players apply pizza toppings to a pizza pie on their way to the top of the Leaning Tower of Pizza.

To begin, each player chooses a particular brand of salami and stores it in his or her backpack. With the salami in tow, the player steps into a lift basket, facing the first pizza pie. A picnic basket of random ingredients arrives on a conveyor belt and spills the contents onto a food preparation table. The player must then quickly match the specific toppings to those that are displayed on the pie in front of them (toppings will also display in an array of flashing colors). Once the ingredients are added to the pie, the lift basket rises to the next level.

If the player cannot match the toppings before the next basket arrives, the basket is dumped on the player, thus ending the game. Subsequently, a large black crow screeches to the player, snatches the salami from his backpack, and gobbles it. Once the salami is consumed, the jackdaw (another of the same species) lets out a horrendous "Burp!"

A successful visit to the top of the Leaning Tower of Pizza adds another pie to the tower. The goal is to build the tower to the moon and then beyond.

Once the added pizza pie appears, the player hangs the salami from his backpack onto a pulley. The salami races back to earth, raising a wicker basket. When the basket arrives, the player steps into the basket and free-falls safely back to the ground. Once back on the ground, a $51.09 bottle of Kedem Sparkling Blush Grape Juice appears, and the corked top goes *pop*!

CHAPTER 4

Being a Banished Being

(Alliteration)

Now that some salami stuff has been seriously settled, please allow me another precious moment for my prognathous (projecting jaw) posture. If you were standing behind me looking into a mirror, you would notice what I mean. I have a pulsating, projecting jaw. It can be quite disconcerting and dreadfully difficult to look at. I used to be quite ashamed, but I learned over the years that sticks and stones can break my bones but names can never hurt me—if I don't allow them to.

My—shall I say—thwarted development is a tick that I developed sometime during the doleful days when boxing was mandatory and headgear wasn't. [Note: Always wear protective headgear when participating in a contact sport.]

Speaking of ticks, it is now ticktock (I'm looking at my wristwatch—yes, I still have a wristwatch), time to tell you how they (not really sure who "they" is) keep us stuck in this stinky structure.

And as I do, keep in the back of your mind that none of us really wants to be here. As I said, we do make the best of it; however, our major is still getting out of here. That is all we think about! I digress.

Once upon a long, lengthy lick (by the way, how many licks does it take to get to the center of a Tootsie Roll Tootsie Pop?) of time ago, Sally Shelly Smith Smythersisserson nearly made it out of here. So as a foolproof measure to keep other such Sally Shelly Smith Smythersissersons from attempts to set same said sail, they installed a crazy high-tech surveillance system.

Honestly, silly Sally Shelly was never really close. What she did was take a bedsheet attached to a broom handle and jump from her second-floor window. Of course, she didn't fly. All she managed to do was fall to the ground and break both legs.

At any rate, we affectionately refer to the elaborate alarm alert as—what else?—Mr. Alarm. Mr. Alarm constantly scans Lasagna Prepoperp's predawn-of-time-like perimeter, looking for prowlers and passersby who might be looking to parole one of us pathetic prisoners. The mighty high walls and mighty wide moats make mighty sure that we do not have a *drowsy sword* of a chance of getting out of here with the seat of our paisley-plaid, tartan-twilled, and swath-stitched pants intact.

Many times have I caught my dungarees on fire while trying to pole-vault over the outside telephone wire. One thing for sure, though: no one has ever called me, "Liar, liar!"

Therefore we have all come to the dismal conclusion that there is only one way out of Lasagna Prepoperp. That being, *yaw on!*

So then, as to our programmed plight in this pungent paprika-like place of perpetuality, please provide patronage as I pain you further with details from past-placed pilgrims.

You see, those of us who were sentenced by fiendish, familial fates must now march, as metronomic allies, through the moldy and mildewed, dank, dark, and catacomb-like corridors of this once prestigious place. There are only a sacred, select few who really know, *really know* (is there an echo in here?), the really real scoop.

CHAPTER 5

Family Feud

One Long Sentence

Here's the poocs. (By the way, it takes exactly three licks to get to the Tootsie Roll center of a Tootsie Pop. That is if you include the chomp as a lick.)

In old-school Lasagna High, a haughty conflict arose between the then upsies and downsies (the upsies are now the righties, and the downsies are now the lefties. I even think that for one brief stint of time, they were known as the innies and outies). At any rate, the whole affair began over what is now a diputs family feud.

The downsies' class president, Cosmo, publicly humiliated the righties' class president, Otis, at a combined class pep assembly. Cosmo reduced Otis to a flame of fury by yelling out at the top of his lungs, "*Sit on a potato pan, Otis!*"

The sharp dispute was a continuation of a conversation the two had had over whether or not the word *potato* ended with the letter *e*.

In a crumpled attempt to cap a molehill from summiting into a mountain, Vice Principal *Pooch C. Oop* summoned both belligerent young men to his oblong office. After calming down both parties, Vice Principal Oop phoned the vice president of the United States of America to get his take.

The vice president of the United States of America suggested that they also involve a local minister from a sizable congregation. "Oh," insisted the vice president of the United States of America, "the reverend must be of a politically correct ecumenical persuasion."

Together, the three-man (no, not PC) restoration committee, in synchronization, formed a charitable organization; and after much consultation, the ill-informed delegation decided upon further consideration to only one's consternation that the letter *e* does not have a rightful place in *potato*; hence, the proud administration posted a declaration that the letter *e* must not be added so as to prove a happy nation. (Whew! That's one long sentence.)

In all actuality, the near ratification was yet in quite a situation when the pizza delivery kid, wearing a *Tahiti hat*, suggested the right answer to their growing frustration. "Why don't you guys just look it up in the dictionary?" was her … "Uh-huh!" sardonic explanation.

So after being made fools of by the kid wearing the *Tahiti hat*, Vice Principal Oop forgot to ring the final bell.

We have been here ever since.

CHAPTER 6

Speak When Spoken To

SWS2!

So then, with no good practical plan for a plausible path of escape, just for fun we decided to speak in quasi acronyms and haiku. We agreed by a majority vote to refer to them as quasicryms.

They are really quite simple to do, yet at times, a bit challenging to decipher. All you do is take the first letter from every word, substituting a number where appropriate, and put them together. "WAZA!" You have a quasicrym. (WAZA = What a zany acronym.)

In addition to being fun and sort of an archaic system known as shorthand, quasicryms can be used as a secret language among friends. "How so?" you inquire. Ah! Inquisitive minds want to know. "IJASAT." It's just as simple as this. Really!

I know, I know, most of you think that I'm telling you something that you already know. But we (the bored students at Lasagna Prepoperp) invented the quasicrym. Not sure what you guys call it. Oh, yeah! Internet slang (netspeak, chatspeak). Well, remember this, TINN JFKTAH KOFTY?

TINN—There is nothing new.

JFKTAH—Just for kicks, try a haiku.

KOFTY—Kind of fun, though. Yes?

Remember: The key to effective quazicryming is relationship. If you don't know the person well, reading quazicryms will be like reading Greek. Unless, of course, you speak Greek.

Quasicryms work best between best friends (BBBF). Hence, the better you know your friend(s), the zanier and less recognizable your quasicryms become to others.

The challenge fun of it all is in the seizing of the unwritten challenge not only to utilize first letters and numbers but to relay information to each other in the form of a haiku. Here is an example of a haiku turned haiku-quasicrym. Mind you, the following is an excerpt from a dialogue between two friends sitting in class, begging the clock to get to noon. Both of the friends are doing their best to keep their shcamots from growling.

Kid 1: W4LT.

Kid 2: YGISS.

Kid 1: YNTA.

Did you figure it out? Probably not. You see, you were peeking in on a private conversation between best pals. As I said, it gets easier and rennuf (Is *funner* a word?) as you develop the language and, more importantly, the friendship. Take a look below. I've deciphered the haiku-quasicrym for you.

Kid 1: W4LT = What's for lunch today?

Kid 2: YGISS = You guessed it—salami stew.

Kid 1: YNTA = Yuck! Not that again.

Told you. Pretty simple. Oh! Punctuation … not really necessary. Especially when you're in a hurry.

One more thing; I almost forgot. It would be helpful for you to know the cadence of a haiku: Five-Seven-Five.

Just remember: 5-7-5. You know, kind of like the combination to your locker.

Oops! Another thing I nearly forgot to tell you (good thing I didn't go to the next chapter). A haiku is an unrhymed Japanese poetic form consisting of seventeen (17) syllables. Have some fun!

Now, give it a try: GHASIALH! (Hint: Lasagna Prepoperp motto.)

CHAPTER 7

Backward to the Main Thing

Drawkcab!

Enough then of Prepoperp gibberish; back to the issue at hand. The issue at hand is why we cannot leave this place of perpetual placement. Here's the simple reason.

It is not just because the final dismissal bell was never sounded (that would just be plain silly). It is unequivocally (quite crystal clear) because, now, most everything here is backward. And since most everything is backward and a lot of things are in reverse, to leave, under present objective conditions, we would have to be arriving.

So it is as plain to see as the booger hanging out of your nose that nobody here can leave. We can't leave because we cannot arrive; we cannot arrive because we are already here.

?ti teG ?ti toG !dooG

CHAPTER 8

Sounds Like She Means It!

Onomatopoeia

Nights at Lasagna Prepoperp can be ex-tr-eme-ly creepy; the old manse can really crack and creak. In the stifling stillness of the wee morning hours, you will hear the most amazing sounds of nature: crickets creaking, bullfrogs beoh-roaking, lightning bugs listing, and katydids stridulating.

But that is not all you can hear. If you lie motionless and learn to block out the sounds of your own snoring, each star-splattered Milky Way night will offer you an additional chorus of sacred sounds.

With your head properly propped up on your favorite puffy pillow, you are most certain to bring into earshot the faint sounds of other marvels of creation. An occasional caw, cluck, and cackle, and an even more deliberate coo, ooh, and moo. Certainly you will be able to distinguish, if you hold your head in a certain way (as if gazing upon a swooshing by of a falling star), a hoot from a howl and an oink from a snort. Oh, yeah! A gobble from a cock-a-doodle-do.

On less than calm summer nights, you will hear tree limbs cracking, leaves rustling, and the wind-driven "rol-is and roo-ms" of nearby misses and faraway wishes of thunder and lightning storms.

Well, needless to say, the "blah, bleeps, and brouhaha" sounds of the upstate night made less than an impression on an annoyed Chloe Clickett.

After Chloe Clickett had stood all that she could stand and could not stand as much as another chirp nor more, the infuriated "bella prepotente piccolo ragazza" (beautiful, tough, small, angry girl) flung off her favorite fluffy comforter and barged, "Swish-swash-swoo-ssh! Whoom-wham-whing! Zim-zang-zing! Boy-ing! Bing-bong-bang … *boom*!" into the unsuspecting lefty boys' room.

CHAPTER 9

The Big Sneeze!

Gesundheit?

The very high-spirited prima donna began boisterously prattling on about her picayune problem. The unrelenting cacophony of Chloe Clickett's rants of sounds and syllables summoned the sleepy-headed boys from their slumping slumber.

In a frenzied flurry to find consciousness, the befuddled boys plopped headlong to the ground. The sudden jolt into semiawareness triggered a unified shout from the disapproving boys: "*Chloe!*"

Unmoved by the state of the boys' disenfranchisement, Chloe Clickett stood her ground, making her presence felt.

However, Chloe Clickett's fury fleetly faded as the pungent aroma nauseatingly penetrated her olfactory senses, reminding her of where she had wandered. The face-twisting odor of stinky socks and smelly feet tickled the tiny hairs in her nostrils. The pint-size princess's flared orifices produced a measure of avalanche-like sneezes.

The boys cried out in harmony, "Run for cover!" The unhygienic brood knew that something of a cataclysmic nature was about to take place. With a slow inhalation, like the silent calm before a storm, time momentarily stood still. All motion ceased; the boys froze in their respective places of shelter (they were under their beds). Out of the corners of their mouths, they silently whispered in agreement, "Wait for it. Wait for it. Wait for it …"

Somewhere between the fourth and fifth "Wait for it," abruptly breaking the quietude, the tenacious little girl erupted into a rafter-rattling series of "Aah-Choos!" One violent "Aah-choo!" after another. The pattern of synchronistic sneezes sounded like a choo-choo train clacking down a track; the boys quietly giggled under their breaths. As the sound of the Aah-Choo Train faded into a series of less impactful little "th—th—th's," a brief calming silence, like the quiet after a storm, followed the display.

One by one, the sneeze-shaken boys peeped out from under their beds. With just the tops of their disheveled heads on display, in a quizzical, singsongy tone, they all sang as one in raptured reply, "Gesundheit?"

CHAPTER 10

The Big Cheese

Isn't That Gouda?

Chloe Clickett called all the sneeze-shocked boys to order. "Come out, come out, wherever you are," the Big Cheese cheddared.

Often referred to as the "Big Cheese," Chloe Clickett (you guessed it) is actually the smallest of the lefties. The tiny-topped taleggio carries a considerable amount of clout, though. All the boys politely bow to her pugnacious persona because, well, in a word, she is so cute!

The mighty mozzarella is simply adorable. She leads her cortege of faithful followers around by the invisible napes of their necks, like a mamma brown bear does with her baby cubs.

The boys are dutifully afraid of the precocious Parmigiano-Reggiano. Well, not really afraid (she's not that much of a Muenster), but because of her cuteability, they let her have her way.

With that said, when Chloe Clickett speaks, her coarse Camembert voice cracks with booming authority. When the Manchego snaps her fingers *click-clack*, the boys jump quicker than *zip-smack*!

So the boys, now fully wide-awake (under protest, I must add), fell into their usual places (like a lineup at a police station). The crumpled glump of fetas stood slouched and side by side at a slump-shouldered kind of attention.

The youngest of the boys shouted in a high-pitched tone, "Dress, right, dress!" The others looked at him with smirks and giggled. The red-cheeked child quickly stuffed a military field manual back into his back pocket.

Unmoved by the feta's feeble attempt to impress the Swiss-spoken Emmental Emmpress, Chloe Clickett clapped into action. "You fellas have to do something about the noise around here at night," she demanded.

Leaving no room for negotiations, the gorgeous Gorgonzola walked down the line of misfits, coco-butting (head bumping) each of them. With a very animated and theatrical flair, Chloe Clickett verbalized each, "Bump. Bump." The delectable, dimpled-dappled darling sounded like someone playing duck, duck … goose.

"Bump! Bump! Bump! Bump! Boing!" She always ended her bumping with a "Boing!" I guess for added effect.

The ritual really didn't hurt; it was more a show of affection than anything else. The endearing expression really did not take very long to complete. The lefty boys' room was the smallest dorm room of them all; there were just five stinky boys stuffed in a poorly ventilated room. So there they were, five slumping Roquefort crumples, standing in a row.

"Well," the small slunk of provolone postured, "what are you boys going to do about all the noise out there?" She sternly pointed toward the window.

But before any of the paralyzed, pimple-faced fetas could answer, Chloe Clickett clamored, "I have a plan!"

CHAPTER 11

Take a Knee

Dim Their Din!

"Mek and Lek, Nik, Hyme, and Ho." Chloe Clickett called out the boys by name. "On with the plan then. C'mon, you guys. Let's go!"

"Go where?" yawned Mek, the tallest of the lefty boys. "What plan?" he further inquired at the end of a cavernous moan.

Ignoring Mek's tiredness (or boredom), Chloe Clickett clacked, "Come closer."

The insistent charmer led the slouching bunch of boys to the window overlooking the candy garden (more on that in chapter 12).

"Hear that?" the little charmer chirped.

A pause ensued as the fatigued friends leaned toward the wide open window; the frogs' croaking roared in their ears like a rocket swooping through a star-splattered night sky. Even the sleep-deprived boys had to admit that the frogs' ribbits could be considered most annoying, "but only if you are awake," Mek pointed out.

Dismissing the tallest boy's observation like one would a hiccup during a pie-eating contest, Chloe Clickett clapped, "Come over here!"

The snap (like a whip) in Chloe's voice drew the boys away from a crisp breeze blowing through the window, which was offering a bit of refreshment to their sleep-famished adolescent bodies. The little tyrant was now down on one knee. The boys knew the drill all too well. Instead of resisting, they all took a knee and joined "El Comandante" in a huddle.

"Can't you guys hear the grinding grunts and glippy glumps?" She overemphasized the *g*'s in the back of her throat.

"Those dreadful sounds are being made by the frogs jumping in and out of the moat! We must put a dim to their din, and we must don the plan right now! Come now, my 'bootlicker' (toady) buds, and I will show you exactly how!"

CHAPTER 12

Miss Crooked Letter's Candy Garden

To See It, You Have to Believe It!

But before I let you in on Chloe's mastermind plan, I must tell you about the candy garden mentioned in chapter 11.

Miss Matilda Coolibah-Billabong taught English here at Lasagna Prepoperp for over a hundred years (or so it seemed). Her teaching methods were quite unusual, but then again, so is everything else here at LP. An English teacher with a heavy Australian accent often made word pronunciations silly and fun.

Over the years she came to be known as Miss Crooked Letter. Not because of the way her posture began to slump over time but because of the way she always said *crooked letter*. There was always a notable high-pitched sound as she enunciated the *oo* in *crooked*.

Miss Crooked Letter, who had a brilliant way of bringing joy to all of us when overpitching the *oo*'s while singing the Mississippi song during a game of jump rope, had Alzheimer's disease.

The song? you ask. How does it go? Not very important right now, but I will tell you: M-I, crooked letter, crooked letter, I, crooked letter, crooked letter, I, humpback, humpback, I. "Mississippi."

So as not to miss the point, which is Miss Crooked Letter had Alzheimer's disease, I must get back to the point. In the old days, many families said that their loved ones were "senile." I remember to this day my Great-Grandpa John had that. Great-Grandpa John always carried around a baby doll. To tell you the truth, I was always kind of afraid of him. I never wanted to get too close because I didn't want to take any chances on catching what he had. I know now that there is nothing to be afraid of and you can't "catch" Alzheimer's disease from someone.

Miss Crooked Letter really was a cool old lady; she was my favorite teacher. Before she became so noticeably forgetful and could not teach anymore, she would often tell us lots of interesting stuff about Australia—"life in the bush," as she called it.

She was a slight woman with delicate features. Really just a little bit of a person but only in stature. In persona, she was a larger-than-life presence. I guess in her younger years she was probably ... I'm quite sure she was, come to think of it ... exactly like Chloe Clickett. LOL!

Though always before telling a (sometimes teeter-tooteringly tall) tale, she would begin by saying, "Class, ready to put on your swag?"

We would, in turn, respond as she came to expect, by singing out, "Swag on!"

Then in the same ritualistic manner, we would all join with her in whistling "Waltzing Matilda."

Interesting, though she was from Australia and still had a distinct vowel phonology (she called it her "Aussie brogue"), she wasn't named after the familiar folk song. She was named after her great-aunt, Maemi Millie Matilda Mae.

In her later years, she would always pause to remind us what swag was. We all never budged, fussed, fidgeted, or begrudged. As she spoke, we all sat, kind of sad, and listened to her as intently as though we were hearing her for the very first time. For a brief moment, she would often drift off in a kind of deep reflection and softly sing, half to herself, "And he sat and he sang, and he watched until his billy boiled, you'll come a waltzing Matilda with me …"

The day that Miss Crooked Letter had to leave, we all stood beside her and looked out the very window that Chloe Clickett called us over to. You know, to hear the "*frogs!*" You can't see me, but I just rolled my eyes and whispered, "Oh, brother!"

Miss Crooked Letter pointed over to where the lilacs were in bloom; she called that enchanted place her "candy garden." Her descriptions of the candies that she saw in the garden were so vivid and so real that we, too, could see and smell them. Even now, when I close my eyes and breathe in real, real … real, real, real deep, I can smell the sweetness so strong that I can identify each flavor.

So from that day on, we referred to that place as Miss Crooked Letter's Candy Garden. There was even a little sign made out of sugar-candy bugs and gummy bears and glops of gumdrops. Of course, we had to rebuild the sign from time to time because the raindrops melted away the candy.

CHAPTER 13

Manichino Ipnosi Rauca

Dummies Hypnotize Frogs

Popping up from the huddle, "Click" (Chloe Clickett's code name while on mission. I know, I know, crack that code. But she insisted.) produced a back-pants-pocket-worn booklet. The title of the booklet was *How to Hypnotize Frogs for Dummies.*

Before commencing to read, Click put on a knitted black ski mask (her disguise). Now that she was incognito, the disguised point person read the two simple instructions.

First, hold the frog in one hand, tummy up. Encircle the frog's chest with your thumb and fingers, just under the armpits, and hold it firmly but without too much pressure.

Second, pet the frog's tummy with your other fingertip, using a repetitive stroking motion from just under its chin to the bottom of its belly. The frog will relax and go into a trance.

Third …

"Oops!" Click blushed, hoping no one noticed. She whispered behind pursed lips, "There is no third."

Mek jumped in. "You want us to do what?"

Without hesitation Click threw each of the boys a knitted black ski mask, along with a backpack.

"You heard me!" the little commissioner quipped. "I want each of you to go out and bring back a backpack full of frogs. Bring back to me every last one!"

Mek took the masks and backpacks and handed one to each of his colleagues.

"Come on, you guys," Mek said. "Let's just do this, or we'll never hear the end of it."

Reluctantly, the five boys took off on the midnight caper to find frogs to hypnotize. Click stood pleased; she had her arms crossed and the black knit ski cap pulled up and balanced on top of her head.

"Now that's what I'm talkin' about," she said.

CHAPTER 14

The Strangest Thing

The Joke's on You!

While in the bog straining to capture the objects of Click's contention, the strangest thing happened. With barely room enough for maybe one more medium-size frog, Mek said, "That's enough, guys; let's go."

Afraid of what could become a very unpleasant outcome should they leave behind as few as one jolly jumper, the other boys said, "No, let's stick around and find just one more frog to please her."

Well, one more frog was what they finally found. Floating like a plump plum in the center of the pond on a lily pad was a smug little croaker. Everything the boys tried to capture the frog flopped at the feet of this jumping joker.

"You can't catch me, you can't catch me. I'm not a frog … I'm a bumblebee."

Instantly before the boys' astonished glares, the ample amphibian turned into a bumblebee and buzzed around their stares.

Then in a glance, with little to no warning, the bumblebee became a dragon flying, dancing around, and storming.

With a swipp and a swoop, a swipe and a swap, the boys' flailing arms begged the creature to stop.

The dragonfly obliged; by just changing direction, it became a butterfly, magnificently clothed, with each color a perfection.

One of the boys shouted, "If I had a net, I could take care of that!"

The butterfly just fluttered and became a tiny gnat.

Brilliant was the solution to the boys' dreary dilemma and really kind of funny. Mek grabbed a frog from his backpack, and *ss-lup*, the gnat was in its tummy.

CHAPTER 15

I Got the Rhythm

Clip—Slap—Clap!

Click stepped back into the boys' room shortly after they arrived with their bundles of frogs all in a trance. Not quite certain of what to do, Click clicked her fingers.

To their astonishment, the creepy croakers (hundreds of hypnotized frogs really is creepy) jumped to attention. Click thought for a moment and then snapped her fingers with a double click. "Click! Click!"

In response to her clicks, the stunned hoppers turned in synchronization to the right (which around here was really to the left). "Just as I thought," she declared. "Now I know precisely what to do."

Click realized that she could turn the frogs' croaks into clicks and lead them wherever her little heart desired. (Of course, now each frog would be referred to as a gorf. You know why.) She turned her back to the boys and entered into a deep state of contemplation.

"A brilliant mind at work," Mek said softly.

"See the smoke coming out of her ears," whispered another one of the boys.

"Yeahhh," came the astonished reply of agreement from the other guys. Click remained mysteriously still as she thought of just what to say.

Then, as abrupt as a cup of cold water splashed in the face of someone having the silliest of dreams, Click started snapping her fingers, clapping her hands, and slapping her thighs in a definite rhythm.

"Click-slap-clap-click-clap. Clap-click-clap-clip-clap-clap-clap. Click-clap-slap-clap-click!" (Try it.)

Instantaneously, the gorfs began to march in place. Once the dazed dancers were all in a row, they began to file out in a very organized fashion. You could even hear the little *slip, slip, slip* of their webbed feet slapping the cold concrete floor.

"Wow!" shouted Mek. "How did you do that? What did you say?"

Click scratched her head and thought about not telling the inquiring minds (you know, inquiring minds want to know). But in a moment of both self-congratulation and a bit of smug enthusiasm, she consented.

"Well," she began, "I just gave them a simple command.

"Go to Righty Hall.

"Don't delay; get on your way.

"So, off you go. Now!"

CHAPTER 16

Invasion of the Gorfs

Zoey Zippett!

Not at all surprised by Click's cunning, Zoe Zippett was slapped from her sleep by the sound of the gorfs' *schh-lomping* down the hall.

"It's Chloe!" Zoe declared. "She must be on another mission."

With a certain zest, Zoe bolted from her bunk and bolted the door, but the bolted door was of little deterrent to the determined pond dwellers.

In case you are wondering, allow me to introduce Zoe Zippett. Zoe and Chloe were identical twin cousins. Yup! You heard me right. Identical twin cousins.

In a strange twist of fate, Mrs. Clickett and Mrs. Zippett (sisters) delivered on the same identical day at precisely the same identical time. For a day or better, there was a real *zip* and *click* of a rhyme; besides, both of their last names ended with a double *t*.

"Crash!" The bolted door exploded from its hinges. The thud of the door smacking the floor was so strong it knocked Zoe off her feet; she landed on the seat of her pantaloons.

Zoe no more than blinked when—*smoosh*—she was surrounded by the gorfs. Looking over the amphibious sea of green, Zoe focused on Chloe. Standing where a sturdy door used to be, Zoe's eyes met Chloe's eyes, and Chloe's smug smirk met Zoe's flabbergasted glare.

Chloe slapped, clapped, and clicked, and the gorfs returned to their predictable midnight rhythmic routine of ribbits and croaks. Zoe rolled her eyes up toward the top of her head and spotted a very pleasant, plump, giddy little green fellow squatting.

CHAPTER 17

Remember Me?

A Wise Little Fellow!

The big bloated fellow sitting on top of Zoe's head let out a behemoth belch. At the disgusting end of the nauseating bravura, toppling head over heels was the tiny gnat.

"Whoa! Am I ever glad to get out of there," reported the exhausted little fella. "I'm switching sides," he declared. "Especially"—he wiped digestive juices from his wings—"after what they've done to me.

"My name is Nitty. Nitty Gnat to you." (Nitty bowed midair.) "And you must be Zoe, one of the identical two?"

Zoe stood to her feet, looking for words. "Yes, I am Zoe. But how did you know?"

"Never you mind," buzzed the little fellow. "We've much to do before I turn mellow."

Nitty was referring to the life span of his species—Culex pipers. Just seven days. He was on day seven, because once inside of a gorf, one day is as seven, and seven as one.

"I will help you get rid of this"—he darted around the room—"bothersome crew. Once and for all, and I will leave not even a few."

Nitty went on to share his situation, though unsolicited. "For, you see, once on the inside of an uncorking gorf"—I'm not too sure what *uncorking* means in this context, but it is fun to say—"the rules say I'm not allowed to change my preordered course. So I cannot turn myself back into one of them even if I wished to do so."

Sadly, little Nitty Gnat landed on the top of Zoe's nose. The mesmerized little plotter looked cross-eyed at her expiring, miniscule colleague.

"Remember, if you will"—Nitty grew weaker—"Miss Zoe, you must. The note left by a dear old friend; in him you may trust."

Zoe thought and thought. The stumped brainiac blew through her lips like a colt meandering up to a bucket of oats and thought and thought and thunk.

"I just can't remember," she cried.

"You have to," blurted Nitty, "or else we're all sunk!"

Zoe moved about, carefully stepping around glumly in the green glumpy-poo. By this time the gorfs were multiplying (you know, like 1 x 1 = 2?).

"Perhaps in the pocket of your blinged-out blue jean. Hurry! You must! I feel I am turning green (feeling sick)."

Zoe continued with zest, looking high and higher and even low. But very soon it was all too much for Nitty the gnat.

Now bereft of her little friend (Nitty died. Or did he?), Zoe remembered. She knew just where it was. The feather-penned note (from an old ancient friend) to befuddle her identical cuz.

CHAPTER 18

A Note from an Old Friend

It's Encrypted

Zoe reached into the left pocket of her Angry Birds pajama top. She always kept important documents there for safeguarding. She fumbled through dozens of documents as the frogs' moaning was incrementally growing.

Pulling out one document after another from her small pocket, Zoe looked like a magic scarf act that wouldn't turn off.

With frogs hopping and envelopes flopping, like confetti flying, Zoe's room looked like the stroke of midnight on New Year's Eve in Pharaoh's palace (Exodus 8).

"Aha! There you are," Zoe trumpeted out in triumph.

Delighted that she had found what she was looking for yet frustrated with her identical cousin, she shouted, "Chloe Clementine Claudine Clickett!" Zoe shook her fist toward the broken-down door and belted out a very defining "Arrrrrgh!"

You see, unlike Chloe, who never seemed to have enough to do, Zoe always kept herself busier than a one-eyed cat looking after two mouseholes.

This day would be no different, except for what to do with the gorfs. Zoe tore open the envelope that read, "In case of a gorf invasion—*Open Immediately!*"

Once Zoe opened the card containing the instructions on how to gain her freedom from the gorfs, as magical as the night itself, she could hear the song "Dancing in the Moonlight." Momentarily, the obnoxious croaking ceased, and the frogs all found partners and began to dance to the classic tune.

(*Stop!* Google the song and dance.)

As "fine and natural" as the tune began, it stopped. You guessed it; the gorfs went back to their brain-numbing barking.

Zoe was furious! With clenched teeth and beet-red cheeks, she read in haste:

Don't you I take mustn't look can will the delay now begin be gorfs may but before at there not another corybantic the to be second and bows find another soon frenzied end relief day!

Roy G. Bip

CHAPTER 19

Friend in High Places

Gnaturally!

"Shakadoobadribbledabble!" cried out an exasperated Zoe. "I do not have time to decode an encrypted note," Zoe further explained as though someone were listening.

To her delighted surprise, someone was listening. Zoe felt a little "Psst!" of air on her right cheek; it was Nitty Gnat.

"Nitty, you're not dead," shouted an exhilarated Zoe Zippett.

"Nope, not dead," declared the little gnat. "I just fell fast asleep. I think you humans call it napalepsy."

"I think you mean narcolepsy," corrected Zoe.

"Yep! That's what I said," agreed Nitty.

Zoe just shot the little critter a confused glance. "But how did you do it?" Zoe queried.

"How did I do what?" replied the gnat.

"How did you beat the gorf rule? You know, the one that said that one day was the same as seven, and seven days like one," Zoe qualified.

"Simple," Nitty replied. "I beat the gorf rule by their own game. I read the fine print in the official *Gorf Book of Made-Up Rules.*"

"Say what?" Zoe shook her head.

"Yesiree," Nitty shot back. "The fine print stated, and I quote, 'If your imagination is vivid enough, you could go anyplace you want to go and do lots of stuff. And if you find someone to believe in you, just for you, you can be anything you want to be … too.'"

So having beaten the odds because the authors of the *Gorf Book of Made-Up Rules* chose a font so small that only a gnat could read it (they never considered that a gnat would read it), Nitty Gnat buzzed with life.

Nitty climbed on top of Zoe's ear, leaned over, and whispered, "What would you like me to be? You know, so I can help with your little"—Nitty darted around the room filling up with frogs—"problem?"

Zoe reached out and gently snatched the miniscule little winged insect as he was about to begin a second tour around the room. (Nitty was imagining that he was a drone on a reconnaissance mission. He even made a louder than usual buzzing sound for added effect.)

With Nitty sitting in the palm of her hand grinning from eyeball to eyeball, Zoe solemnly replied, "I just want you to be my friend."

To that Nitty dusted off his hands together, slapped his knee, and gave Zoe a larger than life green thumbs up!

"Your friend I shall be," he exclaimed with zest.

CHAPTER 20

Jim Dandy to the Rescue

It's a Song!

"There are so many gorfs in here," calculated Nitty. "We are going to have to send out for detangler," he added playfully.

Zoe was desperately trying to figure out Roy G. Bip's code as the gorfs continued to stack up. The discouraged child was at her wits' end with the hairless hoppers and had no room for wisecracks.

"Never mind counting the stupid gorfs," Zoe shouted. "Help me!"

"What's the magic word?" taunted Nitty.

In sheer frustration, Zoe blew a powerful puff of air at the tiny teaser. Nitty began tumbling out of control like an empty fireworks canister falling back to earth.

Instantly, Zoe realized that she had puffed too hard and sprang up in an attempt to rescue the helpless insect from certain doom. In her haste, she slipped on frog goo and fell just short of intercepting her doomed comrade.

Nitty was headed for the gas-fed lantern that had replaced the candlelit wick lamps just a few weeks prior (an attempt to modernize) when he was snatched from his plight.

"Well, Jim Dandy to the rescue!" declared Zoe. "I'll be shoeshined by Shelly who shines shoes at the shoe shop shack." It was Chloe.

"I saw the mess that I had created," confessed Chloe. "I knew I needed to help. After all, we are identical cousin twins."

Chloe Clickett offered a one-shoulder kind of shrug.

"Thank you so much," reciprocated Zoe Zippett. Zoe smiled and nodded. "5 – 7 – 5." She shrugged.

"I know, 5 – 7 – 5," Chloe responded with confidence.

An exasperated Zoe sniffed. She was beginning to cry. "But what does it mean?"

Showing compassion for her cousin twin, Chloe stepped over a clump of gorfs and put her arm around the tearful reflection of herself.

"It's a haiku, Zoe," Chloe tenderly announced. "Roy G. Bip gave you the answer in the haiku formula. Let's try it."

Chloe produced a crayon and a piece of paper and began scribbling. She separated every five words. Then she situated the words into seven rows. Similarly, the whiz kid lined up the words into columns. The solution was found in reading the words (vertically in each column, one through five.

The original letter looked like this.

Don't you I take mustn't look can will the delay now begin be gorfs may but before at there not another corybantic the to be second and bows find another soon frenzied end relief day!"

Roy G. Bip
5 – 7 – 5
The deciphered code looked like this:

Don't	You	I	Take	Mustn't
look	can	will	the	delay
now	begin	be	gorfs	may
but	before	at	there	not
another	corybantic	the	to	be
second	and	bows	find	another
soon	frenzied	end	relief	day

Chloe stood with her arms crossed in delight. She confidently smiled at Zoe. "Got it?"

The light bulb (so to speak) turned on. Zoe replied, "Got it!"

The two girls squeezed together in a tight hug. Together in the warmest of friendship embraces, they shouted out as one, "Somewhere in the rainbow!"

CHAPTER 21

Bunkey

Creature Comforts

Now then, allow me to wander off the trail for just a little bit. What practically nobody knows about Lasagna Prepoperp is that it used to be called Sunny-Side Sanctuary. The sanctuary (most commonly referred to as) was also known as an asylum. An asylum was a place where people with severe and unexplainable illnesses were taken. Many of these sick people went there to die; but in spite of the many horrible kinds of diseases and terrible living conditions, some people lived.

Miss Crooked Letter used to tell us about the days when she worked at the sanctuary. She was very young—thirteen. Her favorite story was about Baby Bunkey Boy. Baby Bunkey Boy (Bunkey) had epilepsy.

Miss Crooked Letter told us that in the old days, many people were afraid of people like Bunkey. They were afraid because they did not know what an epileptic fit was. Sadly, many people today still do not know much about epilepsy.

In the old days, there were many false ideas and assumptions (we all know what that means), which led to fearful superstitions and unkind practices. Miss Crooked Letter said that their fear was based in ignorance (ignorance is no excuse for unkindness)—they were afraid of what they did not know. Kind of like when a solar eclipse occurs. You know, where the moon shadows the sun. In ancient days some people believed that a great wolf in the sky was eating the sun. Sounds silly but only because we know the truth.

Miss Crooked Letter taught us that people with epilepsy have seizures (epileptic fits). Seizures are tiny little short circuits in their brains. The short circuits cause people to convulse (shake uncontrollably).

One day, she explained, Bunkey was having a seizure. Another little boy, named Logan, saw Bunkey all alone and crying. Logan quickly ran and got his big brother Jaden.

Together, the two young fellows went to work providing Bunkey with basic creature (human) comforts (tender loving care—TLC). Jaden kept him from bumping his head, while his little brother, Logan, kept him from choking. Once the seizure stopped, the two boys lay down on either side of Bunkey. They put their heads next to his, and the three of them fell asleep.

While they were asleep, they all dreamed. Amazingly, they all dreamed the same dream. They all dreamed that together the three of them went on a trip. They all went on a trip with Roy G. Bip. (Now I know that you all remember Roy G. Bip from chapter 18. Roy G. Bip is the rainbow.)

The three boys went on a trip with the rainbow ... to the inside of the rainbow. A rainbow going to the inside of itself is not so easy to do, but it can be done. You just turn yourself ... that's much harder to explain. You'll just have to trust me.

Well, a rainbow cannot go on a trip alone, so Roy G. Bip asked his friend Lightning to come along with him and the boys. Lightning agreed. The two danced away into chapter 22.

CHAPTER 22

Somewhere in the Rainbow

Run and Jump and Play!

While the three boys were waking up from dreaming, the next day came. Summoned by Roy and Lightning, the boys hurried. They brushed their teeth, combed their hair, and grabbed a bite of pepperoni pizza pie.

Off they went, hand in hand, on their much anticipated trip. But a trip of this magnitude would not be complete without the theatrics of Thunder in the background.

So, on Lightning's command, Thunder made an expeditious appearance: he bowed a rumble and just as quickly went on his way.

Just for added effect, Lightning summoned Little Rain. "Just a sprinkle," Lightning admonished. "We don't want to dampen their spirits."

Little Rain softly replied, "Just a sprinkle."

The three little boys held hands tightly as they reached the beginning of the rainbow. Quick as a flash, Lightning zapped in. "Hurry now, boys, and I'll show you how it was meant to be and how it should be so."

The very first thing Lightning showed them were the primary colors, standing bold and galore. He turned to Bunkey and said, "Count them with me, please, one to three."

With the primary colors standing saluting all in a row, Lightning addressed the three boys. "There is still so much more that I think you should know."

Just behind the three primary colors, as wide as an ocean, as deep as a sea, and boldly on display, a gazillion tertiary (ter-she-ary) colors were all in a box, perfectly aligned and ready to play.

"The three of you together for today shall be as one," Lightning commanded. "Hold on tight to me, for we shall come awfully close to the sun."

As they stepped inside of the rainbow, Bunkey's seizures went away; he was now like every other little boy and girl, who could run and jump and play.

In an instant Lightning clapped on yellow and blue; the friends joined forces and became a mean green.

Then he zapped a blushing red into the green; it turned yellow once again, amazing for all to be seen.

Playfully, just for kicks, Lightning zipped some red into the yellow. Right before their eyes, "Zowee!" Lightning became an orange kind of fellow.

"Orange? I don't think so," kind of smug-like Lightning said. So he squeezed really hard, and once again orange became just red.

"There is another color Lightning thinks you should know. It is as dark as a dark blue night; it is called indigo," another voice said.

"Oh yes, and last but not least of the colors so proudly on display is violet, but to fit his last name, it is just purple, and so I must say, Roy G. Bip is the name … It's the way to remember the rainbow's spectacular sight. Jumping through the raindrops is the game but most certainly not at night."

Lightning turned to the one who had once again become three. "You are now all charged with potential; learn this song from me."

"Zippity-zap!" Lightning bolted into a song and tap dance routine … It was quite a display.

Somewhere in the rainbow, children learn to fly.
(Tap, tip, tap, tip, tap, tip, tap-tip … tap, tip-tap.)
"Zap!"
Somewhere in the rainbow, big kids cease to cry.
(Tap, tip, tap, tip, tap, tip, tap-tip … tap, tip-tap.)
"Zip!"
Dark days seem so sunny; worries just become funny.
(Tap, tip, tap, tip, tap, tip … tap, tip, tap, tip, tap, tip.
"Zzzzz-it!"
Somewhere in the rainbow, you and I.
(Tap, tip, tap, tip, tap, tip … tap, tip, tap.)
"Zam!"

CHAPTER 23

A Cosmic Encounter

Is It Neigh or Nay?

Meanwhile, back at Lasagna Prepoperp, the two cousins were ecstatic; they jumped up and down like clowns on pogo sticks. "I know exactly what to do," Zoe said as she danced.

Zoe squinted her eyes, grinned her teeth, and flared her nostrils as she found a clearing in the field of frogs. "My dear, dear old friend, Roy G. Bip. I knew ... I just knew that one day you would make good on your promise."

Zoe scanned the early-morning light sky through the only window in her room. The contented little missus dreamily closed her eyes as she took in a slow, deep breath. It was as though she were drifting off to sleep. Actually, Zoe was asleep. Zoe fell fast asleep ... on her feet.

Now Roy G. Bip set his pot (set his pot means that that is where you could find him) somewhere in a place called Tertiary Prismatic. All the inhabitants of TP (TP stands for Tertiary Prismatic, not toilet paper) are known as bows. All bows are heterochromatic (they are varicolored, consisting of different wavelengths and frequencies).

Red was known as Ed, and yellow went by Ellow. Green was Reen, and I think you may have guessed it by now, blue was simply Lue. Together the four colors were an amazing quartet. They sang in a perfect blend as they sprayed the sky and the earth, and a stranger they never met.

One particular encounter I shall save for another chapter. Okay. Okay. Okay! I'll tell you now, but don't forget. After all, Zoe is still asleep standing on her feet.

It goes like this:

Teka-tu was an asteroid who could not be contained; he raced through the galaxy like a reindeer with no reins.

The colors decided that there was something they could do; there was a "dawg-goner" something that would slow down Teka-tu.

As a consensus they asked the sun for a little extra ray and summoned Cosmic Cowboy Comet that one particular day.

Suddenly Cosmic came prancin', on a star named Dancin', with just one thing to say. "Let's get on with it; I'm on my way to Prismythit!"

Dancin' reared up and said, "Nay."

Cosmic made his lasso a ripper; he named it Big Dipper. But no one could see it that extra bright day. As expected, Teka-tu came suddenly, for the others were fun to see; Teka-tu came just to play.

Cosmic let his lasso swirl, the stars all in a whirl, and caught Teka-tu by the welt. Then in a motion like a wave in an ocean, Cosmic sent Teka-tu back to his circumstellar disc belt.

There's not much more that remains to be seen from that bright and sunny day except for a comet, a cowboy named Cosmic, and a dancing star that goes, "Nay."

CHAPTER 24

A Force of Cousins

Big Jerk!

An unexpected early-morning thunderstorm rolled in. The tempest beat violently against the weather-beaten walls of Lasagna Prepoperp. However, the uncharacteristic force of nature lasted exactly sixty seconds. (Don't ask me why, but Chloe always timed thunderstorms.) As suddenly as the rumpus began, it stopped.

Chloe noticed Zoe was still asleep on her feet. Curious, she moved in for a closer look; the better part of wisdom kept her from interrupting her cousin twin from the trance she was in. The longer Zoe remained in her condition, the closer Chloe got. Soon the girls were eyeball to eyeball.

Like the suddenness of an unexpected *pop*, Zoe opened her eyes. Instantly Chloe shot back like a cork popping from a fizzy bottle of grape juice. The terrified cousin twin fell to the ground, scattering some unsuspecting frogs.

Zoe began laughing a boffola of a belly laugh. She had been putting on an act the whole time.

Chloe responded with a resounding, "You big jerk!"

After some huffing and puffing, the girls hugged like sisters after a tiff and got back to the task at hand. The two offered each other a semisuitable high-five and shouted out in agreement:

"Five and seven, five.

"All yous gorfs must needs go.

"Roy G. Bip ... Arrive!"

CHAPTER 25

Roy G. Bip

The Colors Unfurl

In a summer instant, Roy G. Bip shot through the crack in the old single-pane window. The crack was made during a startling mishap; Zoe made it with an unauthorized BB gun. Why did Zoe have a BB gun? you ask. I knew you would.

Well, Zoe always had a crush on Ralphie, the kid from *A Christmas Story*. One Christmas eve, after watching the movie for the tody-toid time, Zoe ordered a do-it-yourself BB gun kit from the Do It Yourself BB Gun Kit Company.

The gift to herself was delivered to her under the notation "A Box of Cookies from Grandma to Zoe." (You know, so no one would suspect.) As soon as the BB gun kit arrived, Zoe slapped it together and foolishly slept with it under her pillow.

Early on New Year's morning, an unidentified bird bounced off her bedroom window. Startled by the *thump* Zoe sprang up from her slumber and shot at the window.

The bird flew off unscathed, but the window had a hole and a very noticeable crack in it. Needless to say, after a good back-to-the-shed meetin' (if you don't know what I mean, ask Pops), Zoe disassembled the BB gun and sent it back to the Do it Yourself BB Gun Kit Company. End of story.

Having been summoned by the dynamic duo's unified command, Roy G. Bip presented his colors. After a few bars of "Pomp and Circumstance," an unfurling of coloration commenced.

Red flowed first and stood proud and at attention. Immediately followed by Orange, it was all looking cool and clean—and groovy, I must mention.

Immediately the two flashed, and suddenly Yellow dashed to Orange's side. Then appeared Green, slightly slower than the others; she looked like she wanted to hide.

The sight was an amazing array, a splendid succession; Blue came through and took his place in the colorful procession.

All the colors stood poised as Indigo made a slightly sinister entrance—dark ... and purplish-blue, not being one to miss this chance.

Last but not least, Purple was called. Strangely, there was no response; the process had stalled.

Then from behind the girls, the most beautiful color of Violet broke through. "All just think of me as purple," said she, "but please know I am Violet O'Hue."

So Roy G. Bip had to change his name—not quite as easy as coming in out of the rain.

But joyfully to all, especially to his purple little friend, he declared, "From this day forward, when you see me, look for the 'V' at the end."

CHAPTER 26

Ella-Ka-Zam

It's Dark in Here?

Simultaneously, Pitch-Black invaded the now achromatic place. All were stunned as no one could see their hand waving in front of their face.

In an Ella-ka-zam instant, it became as black as night. The room loomed eerie and chilled. Even the gorfs squatted in silence. No one dared move a muscle.

Suddenly a deep voice growled:

> I became darkened to you,
> So that what must soon come through
> Will be as clear as the nose on your face.
> Move now, not in fear;
> Gather the last from the rear;
> Bring wholeness to this most sacred place.

It was the voice of Pitch-Black. He offered a word of instruction and then bowed to Light's intervention.

Light replied to Pitch-Black's dramatization. "Here we go again," the illuminous one poked through. "Do not worry, children," she declared. "He is no big scare. Do not be afraid of him when he moves in, because before you know it, I will always be there."

A calming breeze filled the room with a warm illuminating light; the colors were now arm in arm. Roy G. Biv came to the forefront and raised his hands like the conductor of a sophisticated symphony. As he dreamily closed his eyes and slowly lowered his arms, his head followed to one side, like the calm before a storm, and the most amazing thing happened as the colors replied.

Like the swish and swoosh of an artist's brush on a fresh canvas, the colors began to dance.

A series of steplike waterfalls emerged; the cascading colors were swirling, all at a glance.

A low rumble could be heard as the colors crashed together like the churning at the bottom of a great waterfall.

Chloe and Zoe held each other close; together they were brave and stood ten feet tall.

A maiden from the mist suddenly appeared, her arms outstretched in the girls' direction.

They sheltered their swollen eyes from her brilliance and the glare of her starry reflection.

The frogs, too, stood as though in a trance; the bloated croakers arranged themselves in a single file.

The maiden turned and summoned; the frogs began to follow. None veered from the path, not for the next (well) mile.

At the end of the mile, the maiden paused and took her quiet, solemn place; the colors once again could be seen in full array, darting and dancing as in a race.

Well, my friends, the colors were in a race; together they had one more thing to do.

So here is how this story ends.

The End

Frogs at the End of the Rainbow

Who Knew?

Once upon a time the most brilliant rainbow appeared. The bold and blended colors could be seen from anywhere in the world. It truly was a magnificent display, all the colors standing in stately array.

The colors all found their respective places at ground zero (the launch point). It was their unified duty to find a place for Roy G. Biv to set his pot. He had made this very clear: "It is imperative! Every rainbow (promise) must find a place to firmly rest both feet!"

After a very systematic and complicated countdown sequence (Red insisted on beginning at one thousand), the eclectic group exploded into the sky like an intercontinental ballistic missile launching from an underground silo.

The group of seven often referred to themselves as the Serendipitous Seven. They called themselves Serendipitous mainly because it is fun to say. Together, the amazing mixture did display an aptitude for making desirable discoveries by accident. (That is the definition of *serendipity*.) Say it three times fast: serendipitous, serendipitous, serendipitous. Fun!

Well, finding a suitable place for Roy G. Bip to set his pot was no small task. And as the Miraculous Seven (as I prefer to call them) had no formal plan, serendipity would once again be their guide.

Counting backward from one thousand is an awful task; it's easy to miss a step and fall asleep.

At ten the softer color, Violet, was awakened much too fast, for she was just on ninety-nine and probably not ready to make the blast.

The sequence was not to be interrupted; Green was quite a stickler to detail, I'll have you know.

So at five, four, three, two, and one … the others were ready to go.

By the time Violet reached one, the other six were well on their way; she had some catching up to do and could not delay.

Screeching through the sky and quickly running out of gas, detached from the others, Violet knew she would not likely last.

Giving rise to his missing companion, Indigo thought this was just too dark; with that in mind, he nudged Blue, who replied, "Ten-four, checkpoint and mark."

Together the two halted in succession; Green, Yellow, Orange, and Red gave notice and joined the procession.

Halfway, somewhere between here and there, Violet caught up; Violet caught up with not much gas to spare.

Together as friends, bound by a promise, checkpoint was the place they once again found. "This is as good as any," they agreed and dropped serendipitously (miraculously) back to the ground.

Once the Miraculous Seven touched the ground, to their amazement Roy G. Bip had already found a suitable place to set his pot. Amazing! He always arrived first.

"Guess he didn't need us after all." Red rubbed Yellow's head.

"Not so," Roy G. Bip said. "Humanity needs all of you. How else do you think everyone will find their end?"

Encouraged by Roy G. Bip's declaration, the Magnificent Seven stood bold and bright.

Finally, to put a cork in the end of this adventure, hundreds of frogs came hopping over the rainbow. One by one the happy hoppers made a splash in Roy G. Bip's pot. By the end of the day, every last one of the free-flying floppers found its way back to the bog under Chloe Clickett's window.

Of course, Nitty Gnat joined the giddy gloppers as one of them again, and Chloe and Zoe put their differences aside and joined forces to find a way to escape from Lasagna Prepoperp.

The End

Dear Reader,

Well, here we are at the end. I hope you enjoyed the story. You have probably always heard that there is a pot of gold at the end of every rainbow. You now know the truth; there is a pot of frogs at the end of the rainbow. LOL! At least this one.

Thom T. Moht

P.S. The following illustrations were created by Cierra and Logan Weaver. They did their best to show you what I look like.

5

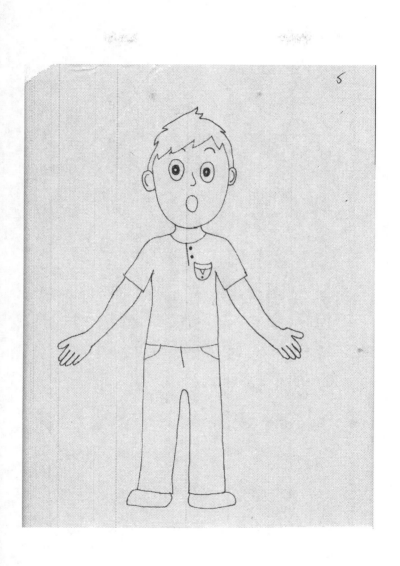

Printed in the United States
By Bookmasters